FRED, AND MARIA, AND ME

FRED AND MARIA AND ME

BY

ELIZABETH PRENTISS

AUTHOR OF "STEPPING HEAVENWARD."

ILLUSTRATED BY WILLIAM MAGRATH

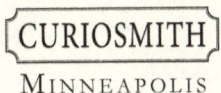

CURIOSMITH

MINNEAPOLIS

Published by Curiosmith.
Minneapolis, Minnesota.
Internet: curiosmith.com.

Previously published by CHARLES SCRIBNER & Co.
in the May and June issues of *Hours at Home*, 1865.

Scripture verses are from *The Holy Bible*, King James Version.

Definitions are from *Webster's Revised Unabridged Dictionary*, 1828 and 1913.

All footnotes were added by the publisher.

ISBN 9781941281024

CONTENTS

ORIGINAL PUBLISHER'S NOTE (1868)

The story of *Fred, and Maria, and Me* originally appeared in the first two numbers of *Hours at Home*. Its quaintness, simplicity, and truthfulness to nature secured it such wide popularity as to create a demand for it in separate form, and, with the consent of the Author, it is now republished.

FRED, AND MARIA, AND ME

————◦◦❦◦◦————

PART THE FIRST

I don't suppose you ever was down to Goshen, in the State of Maine. But if you was, you had the old Avery place p'inted out to you, and heard a kind word spoke about them as had lived there. My father was well-to-do, and so was his father before him. And so when one by one our family dropped away, I was left in the old place, rich and lonesome. At least it looked as if I was lonesome; and everybody was glad when I took a little friendless nephew of mine to be the same as my own child. I hadn't no great use for money, and there's no sense in pretending I knew how to take care of it. Some has a faculty that way and some hasn't. And so it happened that after, Fred grew up and went to New York to live, he got into the way of taking a thousand dollars here and a thousand there, partly to take care of for me, and partly to use in the way of his business.

I didn't keep much account of what he had; and it came upon me all of a sudden one day that I was finding it hard to

get enough to pay my subscriptions with. For I always sub-
scribed to the Home Missionary Society and all them, and
paid up regular; and I wasn't never the one to be mean about
supporting the gospel, either. I paid my pew rent right up to
the day, and our minister knows how often I had him and his
wife and all the children to tea, and how there wasn't never
any stint, and the best cups and saucers got out, and them
children eating until they couldn't hold no more, and a filling
their pockets full of doughnuts, and I making believe not see
'em do it.

Well! I never shall forget the day Deacon Morse come round
to get the pew-rent, and I had to say out and out, "Deacon
Morse, I'd give you the money if I had it, but the fact is, I ain't
had a dollar these three months."

"You don't say so," says he, and he was so struck up that he
turned quite yaller.

"Yes, I do say so," says I. "Fred has been plagued a good
deal about his business, and I've had to help him along; and
then you know I ain't no hand at taking care of money, and so
he's been keeping it for me. And he says I give away too much,
and he shall look out that a check is kept upon me. I expect
that he don't consider that at my time of life folks can't change
their naturs. And it's my natur to keep my money a stirring.
You can't eat it, and you can't drink it, and why shouldn't you
make your fellow-creatures happy with it?"

"But Fred pays the interest regular, don't he?" says the
Deacon.

"Well, I can't say as he does pay it *regular*," says I. "He
sends me twenty dollars one time, and ten another time; and
once or twice he's wrote that he was hard up for cash, and he
knew I'd not press him against the wall. And lately he ain't
wrote at all."

"Pretty business, to be sure!" says the Deacon. "I never thought you knew much, Aunt Avery" (you see I'm everybody's aunt; it's a way folks has), "but I did think you had a little mite o' common sense, if you hadn't no book learnin'."

"I don't suppose I do know much," says I, "and I never was left to think I did. And as for sense, I know I ain't got much of that, either. The Lord don't give every thing to once. Folks can't expect if they're handsome to have sense besides. It wouldn't be fair. And them that has money can't expect to have the gift of taking care of it and hoarding it. No, no, the Lord divides out things even, and his ways are better than our ways."

"I'll tell you what," says the Deacon, "you ought to see a little more of the world. You're a nice little body, and when it comes to standin' up for the Lord, and going round among the poor and the sick, I don't know your match, anywhere. But you're ignorant of the world, Aunt Avery, very ignorant. And as for that nephew of your'n, I guess you'll find *his* gift is the gift of landing you in the almshouse, one o' these days."

"Deacon Morse," says I, "I've heerd you speak in meetin' a good many times, but I never see you so much riled up as you are now. And if it's on my account you're so wrathy, you needn't be wrathy no more, for I've got riches no man can take from me."

"And what if I turn you out o' that pew o' your'n where you've sot ever since you was born, and where your father and your grandfather sot afore you?"

"I don't know—maybe it would come hard. But there's free seats up in the gallery, and if I don't pay my rent, I'm sure I ought not to set in my pew."

"Well, well, I never thought Fred Avery would turn out as he has," says the Deacon. "As smiling, good-natured a boy as ever was! I'll step over and have a word with Sam, if you've no

DEACON MORSE AND AUNT AVERY.

objection. He may think of some way out of this bother. And as for you, Aunt Avery, don't you worry. The Lord will take care of you."

Well, pretty soon Sam Avery came in, looking half as tall again as common, and I'm sure I wouldn't for the world write down all the dreadful things he was left to say about Fred.

"I'll go now and consult Lawyer Rogers," says he, at last.

"But wouldn't that hurt Fred's feelings?" says I. And I don't want to hurt his feelings, I'm sure I don't.

"Besides, there ain't no lawyer in the world can get your money back when there ain't no papers to tell where it went to."

"It's the most shameful thing I ever heard!" said Sam. "And you take it as cool as a cucumber. Why, Aunt Avery, do you realize that you won't never have a red cent to give away?"

"Well, I hope it ain't so bad as that," says I. And I took off my spectacles and wiped 'em, for somehow I couldn't seem to see as plain as common.

Now the next day was Sunday, and I will own Satan is dreadful busy Sundays. And he kept hovering around me as I was washing up the dishes after breakfast, and says he, "How'll you feel a sittin' up in the gallery this afternoon?" Says he, "everybody'll be lookin' up and wonderin', and there'll be no end to wanderin' thoughts in prayer. You don't feel very well, Aunt Avery, and if I was you, I wouldn't go to meeting today. Next Sunday may be it won't be so hard to go and sit in the gallery."

"You needn't call me *Aunt* Avery," says I, "for I ain't your aunt, and you know it. And I'm goin' to meeting, and I'm goin' all day, and so you may go about your business," says I. So I dressed myself up in my go-to-meetin' things, and I went to meetin', but I didn't sit in the Avery pew, 'cause I hadn't paid my pew-tax, and hadn't no business to. I went up into the gallery

and set down in the free seats near the singers. There was old
Ma'am Hardy and old Mr. Jones, and one other man and me;
that was all; and the old Avery pew it was empty all day. If the
people stared and had wanderin' thoughts I couldn't help it,
but I don't believe they did have no wanderin' thoughts. And
comin' out of meeting a good many shook hands with me just
the same as ever, and our minister he smiled and shook hands,
and his little Rebecca, her that used to like my doughnuts so,
she kind o' cuddled up to me, and says she, "Aunt Avery, put
down your head so I can whisper to you." And I put down my
head so she could reach up to my ear, and says she, "You won't
be poor any more, for here's some money of my own that I'm
agoin' to give to you, and don't you tell anybody you've got it,
'cause they'll borrow it if you do, and never pay it back." And
then the little thing squeezed two cents into my hand, and
kissed me, and looked as contented as an angel. And I always
was a fool about such things, and what did I do but burst right
out a-crying there before all the people! But I don't think none
of 'em see me, for they all passed on, and so I got out and got
home, and I laid them two cents down on the table, and I
knelt down, and says I, "Oh Lord, look at them two cents!" I
couldn't say no more, but He knew what I meant, just as well
as if I'd prayed an hour, and I could almost see Him a-laying
of His hands on that child's head and blessing of her jest as He
did to those little ones ever so many years ago. So I ate my dinner, and read a chapter, and went to meetin' in the afternoon,
and our minister preached such a sermon that I forgot I was
up in the gallery, and everybody forgot it, and there wa'n't no
wanderin' thoughts in that meetin' house, I'll venture to say.
Well, after tea I sat in my chair feeling kind o' beat out, and
in walks Deacon Morse. "Aunt Avery, do you keep Saturday
night?" says he.

"Yes, deacon, I do," says I.

"So do we to home," says he, "and it's all the same as Monday mornin' after sunset," says he, "so there ain't no harm a talking of worldly things. And I want to know what you went and left your pew for, and took and set up in the gallery a fillin' everybody's mind with all sorts of thoughts, and a makin' 'em break the Sabbath day a talkin' of it all the time between meetin's?"

"Why, I hadn't no right to no other seat," says I, "and I didn't mean to do no harm," says I.

"If you wern't so good you'd put me all out o' patience," says he. "The pew's your'n, and there ain't no hurry about them taxes, and if there was, why we could sell the pew and get our money's worth. And don't you go to being stuck up 'cause you've lost your money, and making believe humble; the Lord don't like them sort o' things. I don't mean to hurt your feelin's, Aunt Avery," says he—"my ways is rough, but my heart ain't. And what I mean is, don't you go to settin' up there in the gallery, but you sit in the old Avery pew and let's have it look natural down stairs, so we can listen to the sermon and not be starin' 'round, thinkin' to ourselves, If there ain't an Avery up in the gallery!"

"Deacon Morse," says I, "you don't mean no harm, I'm sure, and I don't mean no harm. And I'm sorry I ever told you where my money'd gone. It's turned your natur', and made you kind o' sharp and cuttin'," says I. "And it's turned you and everybody ag'inst Fred Avery, and he ain't to blame for being poor. I'm sure he feels bad enough that he's taken away my living, and we ought to be a-pitying of him instead of upbraiding him."

So Deacon Morse he wiped his eyes, and says he, "It did rile me to see the old pew empty, Aunt Avery, but good-by; next Sunday we'll have things our own way."

After he'd gone I set and thought and thought, and at last I got some paper and a pen and ink and I wrote a letter to Fred, and told him not to feel bad about it but I was pretty well used up for want o' money, and if he could let me have a little I'd take it kindly of him, and if he couldn't he needn't mind, I'd sell the old place and manage somehow. Satan hung round while I was a writin', and says he, "Miss Avery, you'll be as forlorn as old Ma'am Hardy if you sell out. You'll have to go out to board, and won't never have nothin' to give away, and never have the minister to tea. And you was born in this house, and so was your father and your grandfather."

"I'm glad you've learnt manners and stopped calling me Aunt Avery," says I. "And if you're hinting about going to law and such things, you may as well go first as last. For I'll sell this house and give it to Fred, sooner than do anything to please you."

With that he sneaked off, and I finished my letter. In a few days who should come driving down from New York but Fred Avery. He said he was dreadful sorry about that money, but 'twas all gone, and times harder than ever, but he certainly would pay every cent sooner or later, if he had to sell his house and furniture, and turn his wife and children into the street.

"I can't sleep nights for thinking of it," says he, "and my wife can't sleep either, and my little children they keep asking, 'Papa, hadn't we better stop going to school, and go and work for our livin', so as to pay Aunt Avery all that money?'"

"La! do they now?" says I, "the little dears! You tell 'em Aunt Avery won't touch a cent of it, and to comfort their ma all they can, and tell her never to mind any thing the old woman writes again, for she won't have folks kept awake worryin' about her."

So Fred he promised to make all right, and pay me up besides, and he gave me money enough to pay my pew-rent and to get along with a few months. La! I didn't need much! and so all began to go on jest as it did before, and Deacon Morse and Sam Avery left off worrying me about things. But I was turning 'em over in my mind unbeknown to them, and one day when there was only a dollar left, I put on my bonnet and went over to 'Squire Jackson's, and says I, "'Squire Jackson, if you still want to buy the old place, I've concluded to let you have it. I'm gettin' old, and I don't want my affections sot too strong on things below, and somehow my heart feels kind of sore and as if it wouldn't mind parting even with the old place." The fact is, though I didn't know it, I'd got sort o' weaned from this world by Satan's botherin' me and saying, "'Tain't right for Fred Avery to cheat you so! He ain't a man to be depended on!" For if there was anybody I ever did love 'twas that boy, and I never looked to see him grow up selfish or mean; and his last letter sounded kind o' sharp and out o' patience, as if I was the one that owed the money and not him. 'Squire Jackson didn't wait to be asked twice. He jumped right up and went for Lawyer Rogers, and had the papers drawn up, and I signed my name. And the old Avery place wasn't the old Avery place any more. 'Squire Jackson cut down those trees my grandfather was so proud of, and had the house turned upside down, and inside out. I went to board at the widow Dean's, and she gave me her best bedroom, and I tried to make it out I was to home. But 'twasn't home after all, and I couldn't have the minister to tea, nor fry doughnuts for them dear children, and the widow Dean's ways wasn't like my ways, and things seemed kind of strange, and I began to feel as if it wasn't me but somebody else, and my head got to spinning 'round in a way it never did afore. I thought it was the tea, and that the widow Dean didn't make it right, but I didn't like to hurt her feelings by saying that, and at last I said to myself, "The fact is, Aunt Avery, you're an old maid and full of notions, and you've no business sitting here boardin' as if you was a lady; you ought to be doing something as you was brought up to." But when I happened to speak to the doctor about them queer feelings in my head, he said, "Aunt Avery, a journey would do you more good than all the doctors in the county. You've had a great deal to try you, and you've changed your manner of life entirely. It don't agree with you to sit here doing nothing, and you must get up and go off somewhere."

"But whereabouts?" says I. "I never was twenty miles from home in my life, and I'm sure I don't know where to go."

That very day I got a letter from Fred saying he had been sick with a fever, owing to his anxiety about his business, and especially at the step he had driven me to take by his own want of money. "If I had a few thousand dollars I could take advantage of the state of the market," said he, "and make a speculation that would set me on my feet again, and you with me, Aunt Avery. Then you could buy the dear old place back, and live just as you used to live. But alas! this paltry sum is wanting."

"Money wouldn't set them old trees a-growing again," says I to myself, "nor make our old house ever look old again, at least not in my time. But if it could put Fred on his feet again, why it's a pity he shouldn't have it. And I've had hard thoughts I ought not to have had, and called him mean and selfish, and that isn't the way the Bible tells us to feel. If I thought I could get to being as quiet and happy as I used to be in the old times, I'd give him every cent I have left, and welcome. But then where should I live, and who'd take and clothe and feed me for nothing? It takes all the widow Dean's grace and nature, too, to stand having me to board, even when I pay her every Saturday night, and I s'pose people wasn't made to live together; if they was, everybody'd like their tea lukewarm, and not have two opinions on that p'int nor no other."

Just then Sam Avery he came sauntering in, and says he, "Aunt Avery, the doctor says if you don't go off on a journey your head'll split in two, and I'll tell you what, I've got a first-rate plan in my head that'll set every thing straight in no time. You set here all day a worrying about Fred and a pitying him 'cause he can't pay his debts; now if you could put him in the way of paying what he owes you, wouldn't it take a load off your mind?"

"Goodness, Sam," says I, "of course it would. But there ain't no way unless it is to let him have what I got for the farm. And I've a good mind to do that."

"If you do, I'll have you put in the asylum," says Sam. "You don't know nothing about the world, and I do, and I want you to promise me that you won't let Fred have that money without consulting me. Do you think your good old father worked and toiled and got his face sun-burnt and his hands as hard as two horns, just for Fred Avery? What do you suppose he'd say if he could rise from his grave and see strangers rampaging over the old place, and them trees cut down, and them red and yaller carpets all over the floors your mother used to keep so clean and shining? Why he'd sneak back where he rose from in less than no time."

I got so bewildered hearing him talk, that I didn't know what I was about, and I began to think there's two ways of lookin' at things, and may be I hadn't reflected whether or not my father would have liked what I had done. But I knew I'd tried to do as I'd ought, and so I says to Sam:

"Don't talk so, Sam. It makes me sort of shudder to think of my father that's gone to heaven, caring any thing about the old place now, and what color 'Squire Jackson's carpets are, and such things. And if you've got any plan for Fred's good in your head, I wish you'd tell it, for I'm afraid I haven't shown a Christian spirit about him."

"Well," says Sam, "you've got to go a journey and so have I, for I'm going to New York on business. And you can go along with me and see Fred, and tell him you'll take part of his debt in board. That will relieve his mind and his wife's mind, and be as Christian an act as need be. And then, if after trying 'em you don't like their ways, and don't feel to home, you come right back here, and me and my wife will make things agreeable for you. Amanda is a little woman *anybody* could live with, and if anybody could you could. If you like your tea hot—"

"I do," says I, "bilin' hot."

"Well, if you like it hot, *she* does. But then if you change your mind and like it kind of insipid and lukewarm, she'll change her's, and like it insipid. Amanda and I never had no words together, and she's a nice little woman, that's a fact."

"Sam," says I, "you've hit the right nail on the head this time. I'll do what is no more'n Christian, and go to Fred's. Poor man, how glad he'll be, and how glad his wife'll be, and their little children too. I wonder I never thought of it before!"

So the next week we set off, Sam and I, and all the way I kept taking back the thoughts I'd had about him, for it was plain now he had Fred's good at heart; and all along, I had fancied there wasn't much love lost between 'em. "How pleased they'll be, I declare," says I to myself. "I can take hold and help Fred's wife about the work, and them children; and there's my old black silk, I can make that over for one of 'em, if they are any of 'em big enough to wear silk, and then there's my delaine!"[1] I hadn't felt so happy since the day I set in the gallery, but just then we drove up to a very high brown house, and Sam cried out:

1 Delaine—a kind of fabric for women's dresses.

"Wake up, Aunt Avery, here we are!"

"Why, we ain't going to a tavern, are we?" says I. "I thought we was going right to Fred's!"

"Well, this is Fred's; jump out, Aunt Avery, for they're opening the door."

"What! this great palace!" says I, all struck up. "Oh, Sam! it must be they've took boarders."

Sam kind o' laughed, and says he, "Then it'll come all the handier having you," says he.

We went up the steps, and pretty soon they let us in, and Sam pulled me along into a great, long, splendid room, and set me down on a sofy. At first I couldn't see much of any thing, for there was thick curtains over the winders, and the blinds shut to, but after a minute I began to make out the things, and there was a sight of 'em to be sure, chairs and tables and sofys and I don't know what not all in a muss instead of setting regular and tidy up against the wall.

"Things is in dreadful confusion, ain't they?" says I, "but I suppose Fred's wife is a getting supper, and ain't had time to clear up yet."

By this time a lady come into the room, and stood a staring first at me and then at Sam, as if we was wild Indians or Hottentots, and says she:

"You've probably mistaken the house," says she. Sam got up, and says he, "Isn't Fred at home?" Upon that she stared worse than ever, and turned quite red, but Sam up and told her who he was and who I was, and that he was a going down to find Fred, and would leave me in her care.

"But I'm surprised he ain't to home, for I made an appointment with him for just this time o' day," says he, "and it's rather awkward not to find him, I'm free to say."

Just then in walks Fred, a looking as black as thunder, and

he takes no notice of me but just goes up to Sam, as if he was going to catch him by the throat, and says he,

"Well, sir!"

"Well, sir!" says Sam.

And they stood a looking at each other just like two roosters that's a going to fight.

But after a minute Fred turned round, shook hands with me, and says, "This is my Aunt Avery, Maria," and the lady that had been a standing there all this time, she stared harder than ever, and says she, "Indeed?"

Thinks I, she feels bad at having me see her parlor in such a clutter, and so I made believe not look at any thing, but for the life of me I couldn't help seeing them chairs all askew, and so I got up and laid my bonnet on the table, and while I was a doing of it I just set a couple of 'em straight and even, by the window. The minute she see me she run and pulled 'em out and set 'em all askew again.

Fred he kept edging off while we was a moving of the chairs, and at last he got Sam into the back parlor, for he didn't seem to want nobody to hear what they was talking about.

Fred's wife didn't say nothing, so says I:

"Do you keep boarders, ma'am?"

"Keep boarders! *gracious!*" says she.

"I ask your pardon if I've said any thing out of the way," says I. "It looks like such a big house, and as if it had such a sight of room in it."

"Did I understand Mr. Avery to say you were his aunt?" says she, after a while.

"Yes, ma'am, I'm his aunt, by the father's side," says I.

"Most extraordinary!" says she.

"No, dear, not extraordinary," says I. "It's as natural as can be. Jeremiah Avery and Abraham Avery they married sisters.

And Jerry's sister she married a cousin. And Fred's father, he—"

"Good-by, Aunt Avery, I'm a going now," says Sam, coming in, "remember what I've told you about Amanda; good-by,
Miss Avery, good-by, Fred;" and so off he went. And I began
to feel lonesome as soon as he went. And I realized that I was
beat out, what with the journey and all. So I said I should be
glad to go up stairs if it wouldn't be too much trouble to show
me the way.

"Oh, no, not at all," says Fred, and he had my trunk carried up, and sent for a nice, tidy young woman to show me to
my room.

Well, we went up so many pairs of stairs that I was all out
of breath when I got to my room, and had to set down in the
first chair I see. It was one o' them short days in the fall, and
though it wasn't more than four o'clock, it was beginning to
grow dark. So the young woman let down the curtains and
lighted a light, and I could see what a beautiful room it was,
with such a great wide bed, and a white quilt, all sweet and
tidy, and the brown and blue carpet, and the brown and blue
curtains, and all.

"Dear me!" says I, "this room is too nice for an old body
like me. Isn't there some little corner you could tuck me into?"

"Oh, this isn't the best room by no means," says she. "Not
but it's a decent bedroom enough, though. Shall I help you
dress for dinner, ma'am?"

"Why, ain't they had dinner yet?" says I. "I hope they ain't
waited all this time for me?"

"Oh, dinner isn't till six," says she.

I stared at her and she stared at me, and then says she:

"I guess you ain't been much in New York?" says she.

"No, I never was out of Goshen before, till now," says I,
"and Goshen's ways ain't like New York ways, at least I expect

they ain't. But what is it you was a saying about dressing for dinner? Are they going to have company?"

"No; only I thought you'd want to fix up a little," says she.

"I guess it ain't worth while if they ain't going to have nobody," says I. "And I'll jist lay down a little while and get rested, if you'll call me when dinner's ready." So she went down, and I tried to get a nap, but somehow I couldn't, I was so faint, and beat with the journey, and the need of something to eat, if 'twasn't more than a cracker. And when they come and called me to dinner, I was thankful to go down, though 'twas so odd a eating dinner after dark.

We all set down to the table, Fred, and his wife, and me, and there wasn't nothing on it but soup.

"I suppose they economize in their victuals," thinks I, "to pay for living in such a big, handsome house. But I must say I never ate such good soup, and it must have taken more'n one beef-bone to make it, I'm sure."

"Cousin Avery," says I to Fred's wife, "you make your soup beautiful. And you all dressed up like a lady, too. I can't think how you do it. Now when I'm round to work a getting dinner, I can't keep nice and tidy. Not that I ever have such handsome clothes as your'n," says I, for I see her a clouding up and didn't know what I'd said to vex her. There was a man a clearing off the table, and I see him a laughing, and thinks I, what's he laughing at? At me? But I ain't done nothing to laugh at, and most likely it's his own thoughts are pleasing him. But just then he in with a great piece of roast beef and a couple of boiled chickens, and ever so many kinds of vegetables, enough for twenty.

"Why, Fred," says I, "them chickens look as plump and fat as if they'd been raised in the country. I had an idee New York chickens was only half growed. But I suppose being brought

AUNT AVERY AT FRED'S TABLE.

up on a farm you know how to raise them more'n common, don't you?"

Fred smiled a little, but didn't say nothing, and it got to be kind o' silent, and I kept thinking what a number of things was brought on to the table and so much trouble just for me, so says I:

"Don't put yourself out for me, Cousin Avery," says I. "If you make a stranger of me, I shall wish I hadn't come. There'll be a plenty of that cold meat for tomorrow, and I'm partial to cold meat."

By this time we'd about got through dinner, and the man had gone away, so Mrs. Avery she spoke up quite angry like, and says she:

"The idea of my being my own cook and making the soup! Ha! ha! Even John couldn't help laughing!"

"Why, do you keep a girl" says I, quite bewildered. "And was that the girl that showed me the way upstairs?"

"What *does* she mean?" says she, looking at Fred.

"My dear, I am surprised at you!" says Fred. "Of course every thing strikes a person from the country as more or less singular. But here come the children!"

The door opened and in came three children, two girls and one boy, and every one of 'em dressed up in white, with curls a flying and ribbons a flying, and looking as if they'd just come out of a bandbox.[1] There wasn't one of 'em more'n seven years old, and it come across me it was kind o' queer for 'em to talk of going out to get their living, as their pa had said they did, but thinks I they're smart little things and not like the common kind. The youngest one wasn't much more than a baby, but he set up in a chair, and his pa and ma they gave him a good many

---

1 Bandbox—a slight paper box for bands, caps, bonnets, muffs, or other light articles.

unwholesome things, and all the others helped themselves to whatever they could lay their hands on. They wouldn't speak to me, but all they seemed to care for was the good things and the nuts and raisins Fred kept a feeding of 'em with. But then all children's fond of eating, and never would stop if they were left to their own way.

I wasn't sorry to hear the clock strike nine, and to go up to bed. But when I knelt down and tried to pray, it didn't seem as it did to home; there was such a noise in the street of wheels going by, that I couldn't collect my thoughts at all, but I seemed to rush and drive and tear along with them omnibuses till my poor old heart got to beating like a mill-clapper. And Satan he hung round and kept saying, "Well, what do you think of all this? Your 'poor nephew Fred' seems very poor, don't he, and this is a miserable little mean house, ain't it? and don't his poor wife have to work hard? Where's that old black silk of your'n, that you was a going to make over for the children? Hadn't you better stop a saying of your prayers and begin to rip it?" So I got all wore out, and undressed me, and blowed out the light and got into bed. It looked like a nice bed afore I got in, but as soon as I laid my head on the pillow, I says to myself, "Faugh!¹ what feathers! I never slept on such feathers, and 'tain't wholesome."

So I rose up on end, and tossed 'em off on to the floor, but it didn't make no difference, and the air seemed full of brim-stone and sulphur and all sorts of things, such as you expect to smell when Satan is a prowling round. I felt as if I should choke, and then as if I should smother, and turn which way I would I couldn't get to sleep. My head felt worse than it did before I left home, and I began to wish I'd staid there, and not come to this new fangled place where every thing seems so

1 Faugh—an exclamation of contempt, disgust, or abhorrence.

strange. At last I got up and dressed me in the dark, and went out into the entry to see if I could get a breath of fresh air, and who should be coming up but cousin Fred's wife.

"Why, ain't you to bed yet?" says I.

"No," says she, "I ain't, but where does this horrid smell of gas come from? What *have* you been about?" says she.

"I ain't been about nothin'," says I, "only I couldn't get to sleep, and I didn't know what was the matter after I blowed out the light."

"Blowed out the light! Goodness! It's lucky I've got a nose, or you'd have been dead before morning, for aught I know," and she ran into my room and set such a light a blazing that I was half dazzled.

"Don't never blow out the gas again." said she, "but turn it off, so," says she, and she put out the light and went away, and there I stood in the dark, and didn't know where the bed was, and went feeling round and round, and kept getting hold of all sorts of things, till at last I found it, and was thankful to undress and creep in, and hide myself under the clothes.

PART THE SECOND

I got up early next morning and took my things out of my trunk, and fixed them nicely in the drawers, and then I set out to go downstairs, but there was a door standing open, and I saw the children were inside, so I went in, and says I, "Good morning, children," and then I said good morning to a nice-looking woman who was dressing one of 'em.

"Can't I help dress 'em?" says I, for I saw she had her hands full, and up in the corner was a handsome cradle, a rocking away all of itself.

"Thank you, ma'am, there is no need," says she, "I've wound up the cradle, and the baby'll go to sleep pretty soon, and so I shall have time to dress the rest if they'll only behave."

"Wound up the cradle?" says I, quite astonished to see it rocking away with no living soul near it.

"Yes, it's a self-rocking cradle," says she; "we've all the modern improvements in this house. The children's ma ain't very fond of trouble, and so she's got every thing handy, dumb-waiters, sewing-machines, and all sorts of contrivances. If you'd like to go down on the dumb-waiter, I'll show you where 'tis," says she.

"The dumb what?" says I.

"The dumb-waiter," says she. "They're very handy about getting the coal up and down and sometimes folks uses them themselves, if they're tired, or is old ladies that gets out of breath."

"What, to ride up and down the stairs?" says I.

"Why, yes, to save climbing so many flights of stairs," says she.

Well, I'd seen so many strange things in this house, and so many a waiting and tending, that I thought to be sure a dumb-waiter was a man they kept a purpose to carry you up and down them stairs, and says I, "If he is dumb, I suppose he ain't blind, and he'd see what a figure I should make a riding of a poor fellow-creature as if he was a wild beast. No, I ain't used to such things, and I guess my two feet's as good dumb-waiters as I need."

I see she was a laughing, but quite good-natured like, and says she, "The children's about dressed now, and if you won't think strange of it, I'll ask you to mind them a minute while I go down to get their breakfast. I shall be right back. And you, children, you say your prayers while I'm gone."

"Why, don't they eat with their pa and ma?" says I, "and don't their ma hear them say their prayers?"

"Not since I came here," says she. "Their ma don't care about such things as prayers. I make 'em kneel down and say over something, if it's only to make some difference between them and the heathen," says she.

"But they go down to family prayers, I hope?" says I.

She burst out a laughing, and says she, "I guess there ain't many family prayers in this house," says she, "nor any other kind o' prayers either. Folks is too busy a playing cards and a dancing, and doing all them kinds o' things, to get time to say prayers."

I felt so struck up that I couldn't say a word, and I was just a going to run back to my bedroom and look in the glass, and see if 'twas me or if 'twasn't me, when I heard a voice close to my ear say, "Find out if the old lady drinks tea or coffee for her breakfast."

"Did you speak?" says I, to the nuss.

"No, ma'am, 'twasn't me," says she.

Then I knew it was the Evil One prowling round, and no wonder! and I spoke up loud and strong, and says I, "Are you an Evil Spirit or what are you?" "I didn't say nothing about spirit," says the voice, "it's tea and coffee I was a speaking of."

"La! it's nobody but the cook a wanting to know what you will have for breakfast," says the nuss. "I couldn't think what made you turn all colors so. I s'pose you ain't used to them speaking-tubes."

With that she puts her mouth to a little hole in the wall, and then says she, "Find out yourself," and says she to me, "These tubes is very handy about keeping house. All Mrs. Avery has to do is to holler down into the kitchen what she'll have for dinner, and there's the end of it. And it's convenient for the cook too, for cooks don't want no ladies a peeking round in their kitchens."

"Well," says I, "I never." And I couldn't have got out another word if I'd been to suffer.

I went down to breakfast, and Fred was civil as need be, but his wife didn't say much, and I was kind of afraid of her, a settin' there in such a beautiful quilted blue wrapper, and a lace cap and ribbons a flyin', and me in my old calico loose gown. And sometimes when I'm scared I get to runnin' on, and so I kind o' got to talking about the house and the handsome things, and says I, "When I see all these beautiful things, and the water all so handy, and the gas a coming when it's wanted and going away when 'tain't, and the cradle a rocking away all of itself, and them things to whisper into the wall with, why I almost feel as if I'd got to heaven. Things can't be much handier and convenienter up there," says I.

"But when I think again that their ma don't hear them children say their prayers, and dances and plays cards, and don't never see the inside of her kitchen, and all the pieces thrown away for want of somebody to see to 'em, why then I feel as if 'twan't exactly heaven, and as if 'twas a longer road to git there from here than to git to the other place."

Cousin Avery she looked kind o' bewildered now, and Fred, he took up the newspaper and began to read, and he read it all the rest of the breakfast time. And when he'd done, he got up and says he, "I'm afraid you'll find it rather dull here, aunt," says he, "but Maria must take you out, and show you round, and amuse you all she can;" so he took his hat and went off, and Maria she slipped off, and I didn't know exactly what to do, so I went up stairs to my room, and there were three or four women all around the washstand with pails and mops a sopping up the water, and Maria looking on as red and angry as could be.

"You've left the water running, and it's all come flooding down through my ceiling and ruined it," says she, and then she muttered something about country folks, but I didn't hear what, for I was so ashamed I didn't know what to do.

"If the old lady hadn't a left the wash-rag in the basin 'twouldn't a run over," says one of them girls, "but you see that stopped up the holes."

Maria she went off upon that, and I got down and helped dry up the carpet, and kept a begging of them all not to think hard of me for making so much trouble, and they all was pleasant and said "'twan't no matter." When I went down they said

Maria had gone out, so I hadn't anywhere to stay unless 'twas with the children, and I went up there, and the room was all put to rights, and the baby a rocking away all to himself, and the children a playing round, and the nuss she was a basting some work.

"I'll hem that petticoat," said I, "if you think I can do it to suit."

"Oh, no, it's to be done on the machine," said she, "but if you've a mind to baste while I sew, why that will help along a sight. But I'll put Gustavus into the baby-tender afore I begin," says she, "or he'll be into the machine;" so she caught him up and fastened him into a thing that hung from the ceiling, and left him kind o' dangling. So I set down and basted, and she began to make that machine go. I'd heerd of sewing-machines, but I hadn't never seen one, and I couldn't baste for looking and wondering, and the nuss she made her feet fly, and kept a asking for more work, and I hurried and drove, but I couldn't baste to keep up with her, and at last I stopped, and says I: "There's one of them machines inside o' my head, and another where my heart oughter be," says I, "and I can't stand it no longer. Do stop sewing, and take that child out of them straps. It's against nature for children to be so little trouble as them are children are, and they ought to be a playing outdoors instead o' rocking and jiggling up here in this hot room."

"Guess you're getting nervous," says the nuss, "and any how I've got to take 'em out to walk, if it's only to let Mrs. Henderson see that our children's got as handsome clothes as her'n has, if we ain't just been to Paris. Why these three children's jist had sixty-three new frocks made, and their Ma thinks that ain't enough. Come, Matilda, I'll dress you first," says she.

"I don't want to go to walk," says Matilda.

"Don't want to go to walk! Then how's that Henderson

girl a going to see your new cloak and them furs o' your'n? And your'n cost more'n her'n, for your Ma give twenty-eight dollars apiece for them muffs o' your'n and your sister's, and what's the use if you don't go down the Fifth Avenue and show 'em?"

I began to feel kind o' sick and faint, and says I to myself, "If their Ma don't see to her children I don't know as I oughter expect the Lord to, but if He don't they'll be ruined over and over again."

"I'll go out and walk with you and the children if you ain't no objections, nuss," says I.

"No," says she, "I ain't no objections if you'll put on your best bonnet, and fix up a little."

So I dressed me, and I took the girls and she took the baby, and we walked up and down the Fifth Avenue, and I heerd one nuss say to our'n:—

"Is that your new nuss?" says she.

"La! no, it's our *aunt,*" says she, and then they both burst out a laughing.

Well, it went on from day to day that I hadn't anywhere else to stay, and so I stayed with them children. And Fanny, the oldest one, she got to loving me, and nothing would do but she must sleep in my bed, so I had her in my room, and I washed and dressed her, and I told her stories out of the Bible and Pilgrim's Progress, and taught her hymns; and then Matilda she wanted to come, too, and they moved her little bedstead in, and she slept there, and so by degrees I got so that you couldn't hardly tell me from the nuss. And it was handy for her to have me stay home every Sunday afternoon and see to the children while she went to meetin' and home to see her folks, and she said so, and that she felt easy to leave 'em with me, because I'd know what to do if anything happened to 'em. And it got to be handy for her to call me if the baby cried more'n common in the night, or if he had the croup. For Gustavus was a croupy child, and every time his Ma had company, and would have him downstairs with his apron took off, so as to show them white arms and them round shoulders of his, full o' dimples, why he was sure to wake up a coughing and scaring us out of our wits. Well, I wasn't young and spry as I used to be, and it's wearing to lose your sleep o' nights, and then Fred's ways and Maria's ways made me kind o' distressed like, and Sam Avery he kept writing and hectoring me, and saying I ought to have the law of Fred, and Satan he roared round some, and all together one night after dinner, just as we was a getting up from the table, I was took with an awful pain in my head, and down I went flat on to the floor. Fred he got me up, and they sent for the doctor, and the doctor he questioned this one and he questioned that one, and he said nusses' places wasn't places for old ladies, and, then again, plenty of fresh air was good for old ladies, and to have things pleasant about 'em, and to be took round and diverted. So I was sick a good while, and I expect I made a sight of trouble, for one day they was all a sitting round in my room, and little Fanny she stood by the side of the bed, and says she, "Aunt Avery, what is a Regular Nuisance?"

"I don't know," says I, "I never saw one. 'Tain't one of the creeturs in Pilgrim's Progress, is it?" says I.

"For Ma says you are a Regular Nuisance," says she.

"You naughty girl, how dare you tell such stories?" said her Ma, and she up and boxed the little thing's ears until they were red.

"It ain't a story, and you did say so. You told Mrs. Henderson—"

"Hold your tongue, you silly little goose!" said Fred. "Don't mind her, Aunt Avery, she's nothing but a child."

"They do say children and fools speak the truth," says I, "and maybe you think I'm a fool; and maybe I am. But I ain't deaf nor blind, and I can't always be dumb. And I won't deny it, Fred, I've had hard thoughts towards you. Not about the money; I don't care for money, and never did. But it's so dreadful to think of your saying you was poor when you wasn't poor, and all those things about your little children a going out to work for their living."

"Pshaw! that was a mere joke," cried Fred. "You knew, as well as I did, that they were only a parcel of babies."

"Well, and there's another thing I want to speak of. Did Sam Avery coax me to come here because he thought it would take a weight off your mind; or because he thought it would plague you and Maria to have a plain old body like me round the house?"

"Sam Avery be hanged!" said Fred. "The fact is, Aunt Avery, I ain't worse than other men. I was in love with Maria, and I was determined to have her. And I wanted her to live with me pretty much as she had been used to living. If you think this is too fine a house for her to possess, why you'd better go and examine the one she was born and brought up in. I economize all I can; we don't keep a carriage, and Maria has often to ride in stages, and pass up her sixpence like any old washerwoman. And I deny myself about giving. I give nothing to the poor, and subscribe to no charities, except charity balls; and Sam Avery, a sanctimonious old sinner, has just give five hundred to Foreign Missions. If it wasn't for being twitted about the money I had from you, I could hold up my head as high as any man. But since you've been and set all Goshen on to me, why my life is a dog's life, and little more."

It cut me to the heart to think I'd kept him so short of

money that he hadn't nothing to give away.

"Well," says I, "you'll soon have the value of the old place, and be out of debt, besides. For I'm going where I shall want none of those things."

Just then I looked up, and there was Maria standing in front of Fred, her face white and her lips trembling. She had gone out with the child, and we hadn't noticed she'd come back.

"Do you mean to say you've been borrowing money of this old woman, and have been deceiving me all along by pretending she gave it to you? Look me in the face, then, if you dare!"

"What a fuss about a few thousand dollars!" returned he. "Of course I expect to repay her all she's let me have. And you, Maria, are the last person to complain. Was not this house your own choice? And how did you suppose a man of my age could afford to buy it without help?"

Maria made no answer. It seemed as if all her love for him had turned into contempt.

I riz up in the bed, as weak as I was, and says I, "Fred Avery, come here to me, and you, Maria, come here too, and you two kiss each other and make up, right away, or I shall die here in this house, and can't have my own minister to bury me, and shall have to put up with your'n. Why, what's money when you come to putting it along side of dwelling together in unity? Quick, get a paper, and let me sign it; and say in the paper it was my free gift, and I never lent none of it; and, oh hurry, Fred, for I feel so faint and dizzy!"

"I believe you've killed the poor old soul!" said Maria, and she fanned me, and held salts to my nose, and tried to make me lie down. But I wouldn't, and kept making signs for the paper, for I thought I was going to drop away in no time.

"Get the paper this instant, Fred," said Maria, pretty much

as if he was one of the children. So he went and got it, and I signed my name, and then I lay back on the pillow, and I don't know what happened next, only I felt 'em fanning me, and a pouring things down my throat; and one says, "Open the window!" and another says, "It's no use!" and then I heard a child's voice set up such a wail that my old heart began to beat again, and I opened my eyes and there was little Fanny, and she crept up on to the bed, and laid her soft face against mine, and said, "You won't go and die, Aunt Avery, and leave your poor little Fanny?" and I knew I mustn't go and leave that wail a sounding in her Ma's ears. And when I know I ought not to do a thing, I don't do it. So that time I didn't die.

Well! it's an easy thing to slip down to the bottom of the hill, but it ain't half so easy to get up again as it is to lay there in a heap, a doing nothing. And it took a sight of wine whey, and calves' feet jelly, and ale and porter, and them intemperate kind of things to drag me a little way at a time back into the world again. I didn't see much of Fred, but Maria used to come up and sit in my room, and work on a little baby's blanket she was a covering with leaves and flowers, and sometimes she'd speak quite soft and gentle like, and coax me to take my beef-tea, just as if she wanted me to get well. She wasn't never much of a talker, but we got used to each other more'n I ever thought we should. And one day—there! I know it was silly, but when she was giving me something, I took hold of that pretty soft hand of hers and kissed it. And the color came and went in her face, and she burst out a crying, and says she:

"I shouldn't have cared so much, only I *wanted* to love Fred!"

That was all she ever said to me about him after I'd signed that paper, but when folks' hearts are full they ain't apt to go to talking much, and I knew now that Maria had got a heart, and that it was full, and more too.

At last I got strong enough to ride out, and Maria went with me, and after a while she used to stop at Stewart's and such places to do her shopping, and I would stay in the carriage until she got through. I wanted to see what sort of a place Stewart's was, for I heerd tell of it many a time, but I thought Maria wouldn't want to have me go in with her, and that maybe I could go some time by myself. I asked her what they kept there, and she said, "Oh, *every*thing," and I'm sure the shop looked as big as all out doors. She used to get into a stage sometimes to go down town, and I watched all she did in them stages, so as to know how to manage, and one day I slipped out and got into the first one that came along, for, thinks I, why shouldn't I go to Stewart's if I've a mind, all by myself?

It carried me up this street and across that, and at last it stopped near a railroad depot, and all the passengers but me got out. I waited a little while, and at last I got up, and says I to the driver, "Ain't you a going no further?"

"No, I ain't," says he.

"But I want to go to Stewart's," says I.

"I've no objections, ma'am," says he, and began to beat his arms about, and blow his hands, as if he was froze. I didn't know what to do, or where I was, but pretty soon he turned his horses' heads about, and began to go back the very way we'd come. So I pulled the check, and says I, "I want to go to Stewart's."

"Well, *ain't* you going?" says he, "and I don't know as there's any need to pull a fellow's leg off!"

"I beg your pardon, I didn't mean to hurt you," says I, and with that I sat down, and we rode and rode till we got into Broadway, and then I began to watch all the signs on the shops, so as to get out at the right place. At last we got most down to the ferries, so I asked a man that had got in if we hadn't passed Stewart's.

"Oh yes, long ago," says he.

"Dear me, I must get out, then," says I. "I told the driver I wanted to go there, but I suppose he has a good deal on his mind a picking his way along, and so forgot it." So I got out and began to walk up the street, and I ran against everybody and everybody ran against me, and I came near getting run over a dozen times, and was so confused that I didn't rightly know how far I'd walked, so I stopped a girl, and says I, "Oh, do you know where Stewart's is?"

"La, it's three or four blocks down so," says she.

"I didn't see no sign up," says I, "and so I passed it."

"I guess you'll have to look till dark if you're looking for signs," says she, and away she went. I was pretty well used up, I was so tired, but I went back, and this time I found it and went in. The first thing I asked for was tape. "We don't keep it," says the clerk.

"Do you keep fans?" says I.

"No, fans are not in our line."

"Well, have you got any brown Windsor soap?"

No, they hadn't got any kind of soap. There was some other little things I wanted, such as pins, and needles, and buttons, but I didn't like to ask for 'em, for if they didn't happen to have none of 'em, it might hurt their feelings to have people know it. But there was one thing I thought I'd venture to ask for, and that was a velvet cloak. I'd heerd Maria say a new kind of spring cloak was uncommon handy, and I had twenty dollars in my pocket a purpose to buy it with. For I kind o' liked Maria, and I pitied her too, for she and Fred didn't seem good friends, and then I had made so much trouble when I was sick.

The clerk said yes, they had some, but, says he, "They're very expensive," and never offered to show them to me. Well, I ain't perfect, and I felt a little riled in my feelings. And says I, as mild as I could, "I didn't say nothing about the price. I asked you if you'd got any o' them cloaks." Upon that he took out one or two, and I liked them pretty well, though when I heerd the price I found my twenty dollars warn't agoing to help much; but then I didn't care. "I don't want no such finery myself," thinks I, "but Maria's young and she wants it, and she and Fred feel pretty bad, and I don't know as it's any of Sam Avery's business how I spend my money. Folks down to Goshen they might say Aunt Avery she's grown worldly and fond of the pomps and vanities, but then 'tain't true if they do say it. 'Tain't worldly to wear good clothes, and 'tain't pious to wear bad ones. The Lord don't look on the outside, and I have a feeling that it's right for Maria to have one o' them cloaks." So I says to the man, "Won't you be so good as to let me carry home two o' them cloaks to show Mrs. Avery, for I don't know which of 'em she'd like best." He stared at me half a minute, and then says he, "Are you her seamstress?"

"No, I ain't," says I. "I suppose you think there ain't no ladies but what wears silks and satins, and laces, and velvets. But I'll tell you what, Abijah Pennell, when you've lived in this world as long as I have you won't judge folks jest by their clothes."

He colored up and looked at me pretty sharp, and says he, "Excuse me for not recognizing you, Miss Avery. It's so many years since I left Goshen. I'll send the cloaks for you with pleasure. Won't you have one for yourself?"

"No, Abijah, no," says I, "them 'ere cloaks ain't for old women like me." So I bid him good-by, and all the clerks good-by that stood round a laughing in their sleeves, and I

went out to look for a stage, and there was a nice policeman a
standing there, so I told him where I wanted to go, for, thinks
I, it makes a good deal of odds which stage you get into, and
he put me in, and I sat down by a man with a gold ring on his
finger, and little short, black curls round his forehead, and he
was quite sociable, and I told him where I'd been, and how I
hadn't bought nothing, and then we talked about the weather,
and at last he got out. And just after that I put my hand into
my pocket to get at my purse, and there wasn't no purse there.

"Goodness!" says I to all the folks in the stage, "my purse
ain't in my pocket!"

"That man with the curly hair sat pretty close to you," says
one of the passengers. "But it's no use trying to catch him now."

"But I ain't got no money to pay my fare," says I, "and I
must get right out." So I made the driver stop, and says I, "I'm
very sorry, Mister, but my pocket's been picked and I can't pay
my fare."

"You don't come that dodge over me, old woman," says he.
"If you can't pay your fare you'd better git out and walk." So I
got out and walked till I was ready to drop, but when I went
in, there was Maria admiring of them cloaks, and says she:

"Aunt Avery, somebody's sent me these cloaks to choose
which I'll have, and I'm afraid it's Fred. And Fred's not going
to make up with me with cloaks, I can tell him."

"No, dear," says I, "it ain't Fred, it's your old aunt, that
wants to see you pleased and happy, and that's went down to
Stewart's and picked out them cloaks."

"La! I never!" says she, "I thought you had an idea that
everybody ought to wear sackcloth and ashes." But she did
seem sort of pleased and grateful, and Fred did too, when he
came home, and he and Maria behaved quite decent to each
other, but I could see there was something on their minds, and

that they weren't good friends by no means.

Little Fanny, she and I kept together a good deal, for she wasn't no care, and Gustavus, he got to be hanging around his old aunt, and I taught him to come in every night to say his prayers. That night he was so good, and coaxed so prettily to sleep with me, that I thought I wouldn't care if the doctor did scold, the dear child should have his way now and then. And seeing the little creature a lying there so innocent and so handsome, and a looking jest as Fred used to look, I couldn't help praying more'n common for him, and says I to myself, "He won't have the croup tonight, any how, with me to cover him up and keep him warm." But about two o'clock I was woke out of a sound sleep with that 'ere cough of his. It went through me like a knife, and I got up and gave him his drops right away, and put on more coal, and covered him up warmer, but he didn't seem no better, so I had to go and call Fred to go for the doctor.

Well! well! there's some has to toil and fight, and work their way up hill toward the heavenly places, and there's some that never know nothing about no kind o' battling, and their little white feet never go long enough over the dusty road to get soiled or tired. And when the daylight came in at my windows that morning, Fred and Maria was good friends again, and he had his arms around her, and she clung close to him, but little Gustavus was gone. Gone where such dreadful words as money ain't never mentioned; gone straight up to the great white throne without no fears and no misgivings! Oh, Fred, you're a rich man now, for you've got a child up in heaven.

That night Maria had the children kneel down and say their prayers in her room, but I never see her shed no tears, nor heard her a grieving. She hid her poor broken heart away in her bosom, and there wan't no getting at it to comfort it. I

DEATH OF LITTLE GUSTAVUS.

couldn't but lay awake nights a hearing of her a walking up and down in her room, and a chafing and a wearing all to herself, and them tears she couldn't shed was a wetting my pillow and fairly a bathing my poor prayers for her.

We had an early spring this year, and Fred said the doctor told him I'd better not stay in New York till warm weather came. So I wrote to Sam Avery, and told him I was a coming home in May, and I thought I ought to tell him how I'd gone contrary to his advice, and signed away all I'd ever lent Fred, and made him a life member of the Bible Society and them. And I asked him not to feel hard to me, and to see that the Widow Dean had my room ready against I got back. Maria was stiller than ever, and hardly ever talked at all, and Fred looked full of care, and yet more as he used to when he was a boy. And we parted kindly, and Maria as good as said she was sorry to have me go, only it was time to take the children out of town. Fanny, she said she was a going with me, and she got a little trunk and put her things in it, and was as busy as a bee folding and packing. And when I saw her heart so set upon it, I felt a pang such as I never felt before, to think I hadn't got no home to take her to, and how it wouldn't do to venture her on the Widow Dean, who couldn't abide children. Well! her Pa had to carry her off by main force when the carriage came, and I had a dull journey home, for I didn't seem to have no home, only the name of one. For I never took to boardin'.

It was past five o'clock when I got to Goshen post-office, and thinks I, Sam Avery won't be upbraiding of me tonight, for it's quite a piece from his house over to the Widow's. But who should I see a waiting there but Sam and his shay.[1]

"How d'ye do? Aunt Avery, glad to see you home again," says he, "jump right into the shay and I'll get your trunk.

1 Shay—a two-wheeled carriage drawn by one horse.

Amanda, she's waiting tea for you, and I rather think you'll find it bilin' hot," says he.

"But I was a going to the Widow Dean's," says I.

"Don't talk no Widow Dean's to me," says Sam, "but you jest get into that shay o' mine and go where you're took to, Aunt Avery."

And how nice and clean and shiny Amanda's house did look, to be sure! And how she kissed me, and said over and over 'twas good to get me home again. And how that tea did build me up, and make me feel young and spry as I used to feel in old times.

Well, after tea I put on an apron she lent me, and she and me we washed up and cleared away, and Sam, he read a chapter, and we had prayers, and I went to bed, and I never knew nothing after I laid my head on the pillow, but slept all night like a little baby.

At breakfast, I expected Sam would begin about Fred, but he didn't, and Amanda she didn't; and we two we washed up the dishes and swept the floors, and made the beds, and Amanda she let me do jest as I was a mind to, and it didn't seem like boardin' at all. And after a while I left off expecting Sam to hector me about Fred, and got to feeling easy in my mind. And we had the minister to tea, and his wife and children, and you never saw nobody so pleased as they was at their things. For of course I wasn't going to New York without getting a black silk gown for my minister's wife, and a doll for little Rebecca, and wooden cats and dogs for the rest of 'em. Sam Avery he was a going and a coming more'n common this spring, and he says to me one day, "Aunt Avery, don't you go to looking at the old place when you're wandering out. You see Squire Jackson's been a cutting and a hacking, and there's a good deal going on there, and it might rile your feelings to see the muss," says he.

So I didn't go near the old place, and I didn't want to, and the time it slipped by and I got to feeling that nothing aggravating hadn't never happened to me. Folks come for Aunt Avery when they was sick, jest as they used to, and the minister he dropped in every now and then, and Deacon Morse he had over plenty of them rough sayings of his that didn't mean nothing but good-will, and so I felt quite to home. There wasn't but one thing a stinging of me, and that was Fred and his ways, and Maria and her ways. And I kind o' yearned after them children, and couldn't help a thinking, if I hadn't been and sold the old place, there'd always been a home for them in the summer time, and a plenty of new milk and fresh eggs.

Well! it got to be well on into July, and one afternoon Sam Avery he come in, and says he, "Aunt Avery, you put on your bonnet and get into the shay and go right down to the old place. There's somebody down there wants looking after," says he.

"Dear me, is any of 'em sick?" says I. And I put on my things, and Sam whipped up the old horse, and next news, we was driving up to the house. Things didn't look so changed after all. Them trees was gone, there's no denying of it, but there wasn't nothing else gone, and when I went in there wasn't none o' Squire Jackson's red and yaller carpets on the floors, nor none o' his things a laying about. But there was my little light-stand a setting in the corner, and my old Bible on it, with the spectacles handy, jest as they used to be, and our cat she come a rubbing of herself against me, as much as to say, "Glad to see you back, Aunt Avery," and then two little children, they come running up, and one kissed me and the other hugged me, and 'twas Fanny and Matildy, and then Fred Avery he walks up, and says he, "Welcome home, Aunt Avery!" and Maria she takes both o' my old hands and a squeezes of 'em up to her heart, and then says she, "Here's our new baby come to see you, and her name's Aunt Avery," says she, and she put it into my arms, and 'twasn't bigger than a kitten, but it had a little mite of a smile a shining on its face all ready a waiting for me. By this time I was a'most beat out, but they set me down in my old chair, and them children they was round me, and Fred a smiling, and Maria a smiling, and Sam Avery a shaking hands with everybody, and I didn't pretend to make nothing out o' nobody, for I knew 'twasn't nothing real, only something I was reading out of a book. Only that 'ere little baby that was named Aunt Avery, it held tight hold o' one o' my fingers with its tiny little pink hand, and that wasn't nothing you could read out of a book, no how. And then Amanda she opened the door into the big kitchen, and there was a great long table set out with my best china and things, and our minister and his wife, and all them children, and Deacon Morse and the Widow Dean, they'd come to tea. And the minister he stood up, and says he, "Let us pray." And in his prayer he told the Lord all about it, though I guess the Lord knew before, how Maria had made Fred sell that big house of his, and how he'd bought me back the old place, and how we was all come to tea, and a good many other things I couldn't rightly hear for the crying and the sobbing that was a going on all around. And then we had tea, and I never thought when Amanda made me fry all them doughnuts and stir up such a sight o' cake what 'twas all a coming to, for it's my opinion that nobody knows when they does a thing, what's a going to come next, though the Lord he knows all along.

Well, it begun to grow dark, and one after another they all come and bid me good-night, till at last everybody was gone but me and Maria, and them children of hers. And Maria came up to me, and says she, "Does the old place look pleasant, Aunt Avery?" but I couldn't answer her for them tears that

AUNT AVERY AT HER OLD HOME.

kept a choking me. And so she said if I didn't mind, and it wouldn't be too much trouble, she wanted to stay with me the rest of the summer, till Fred could get a new, honest home for her somewhere else. Wasn't that just like an angel now, after all the trouble I'd been and made for her, a setting of her against her husband, and a turning of her out of her beautiful house and home, and a making her buy back for me my old place? So she and me we undressed them children, and made them kneel down and say their prayers, and we put them to bed upstairs, and I began to feel to home.

And Maria she staid till cold weather came, and she sat and read my old Bible, and talked to them children about the place Gustavus had traveled to, and she paid respect to our minister, and wiped up the china when I washed it, and fitted her ways to my ways quite meek and quiet-like.

And Fred paid back every cent he'd borrowed, for he'd kept account, and knew all about it, and he started fair and square in the world again, owing nothing to nobody. So now I've a home for him and Maria and the children, and the old house is full of Averys once more, and so is the old pew, and all the taxes paid up regular.

So you are a rich man now, Fred, and you're a rich woman, Maria, for you've got a child up in heaven!

MAN'S QUESTIONS & GOD'S ANSWERS

Am I accountable to God?
"Every one of us shall give account of himself to God." (Romans 14:12).

Has God seen all my ways?
"All things are naked and opened unto the eyes of Him with whom we have to do." (Hebrews 4:13).

Does He charge me with sin?
"The Scripture hath concluded all under sin." (Galatians 3:22).
"All have sinned." (Romans 3:23).

Will He punish sin?
"The soul that sinneth, it shall die." (Ezekiel 18:4).
"For the wages of sin is death." (Romans 6:23).

Must I perish?
"God is not willing that any perish, but that all should come to repentance." (2 Peter 3:9).

How can I escape?
"Believe on the Lord Jesus Christ, and thou shalt be saved." (Acts 16:31).

Is He able to save me?
"He is able also to save them to the uttermost that come unto God by Him." (Hebrews 7:25).

Is He willing?
"Christ Jesus came into the world to save sinners." (1 Timothy 1:15).

Am I saved on believing?
"He that believeth on the Son hath everlasting life." (John 3:36).

Can I be saved now?
"Now is the accepted time; behold, now is the day of salvation." (2 Corinthians 6:2).

As I am?
"Him that cometh to Me I will in no wise cast out." (John 6:37).

Shall I not fall away?
"Him that is able to keep you from falling." (Jude 24).

If saved, how should I live?
"They which live should not henceforth live unto themselves, but unto Him which died for them." (2 Corinthians 5:15).

What about death, and eternity?
"I go to prepare a place for you; that where I am, there ye may be also." (John 14:2, 3).

www.ingramcontent.com/pod-product-compliance
Lightning Source LLC
Chambersburg PA
CBHW020320150626
46552CB00022B/3040